EIGHT

THE TAROT
TRILOGY
BOOK TWO

# of CUPS

J.D. BRETTON

EIGHT OF CUPS

THE TAROT TRILOGY, BOOK TWO

J.D. Bretton

Printed in the United States of America

First Printing May 2017

Splintered Sky Publishing

ISBN 978-0-9974682-4-3

Cover Design by Fiona Jayde
Interior Design by The Deliberate Page

For H.R.-
Thanks for the inspiration

"Of all ghosts the ghosts of our old loves are the worst."

The Gloria Scott
Sir Arthur Conan Doyle

CHAPTER 1

The sweet stench of memory twisted inside her, each inhale muddy and thick with regret. Xavier's dark, sorrowful eyes haunted her. Danielle remembered the touch of his hair against her skin, her hands tracing the wing tattoo on his neck, his lips on hers, their bodies entwined.

She had dropped her heart on the doorstep of the house when she left.

She would not return to reclaim it.

Danielle threw back three mini-bottles of vodka, not bothering with the plastic cup the flight attendant gave her. The liquor burned her lips and throat. She relished the numbness that washed over her and prayed for an escape from the nightmares that played in an endless rewind in her head.

She would arrive in Aguadilla, Puerto Rico in a few hours. As she settled into her seat, the tarot card she had shoved in her front pocket jabbed into her — the Eight of Cups. It signified escape, abandonment, withdrawal: all the things she felt at this moment. The man on the card turned his back on everything and walked across the water, alone. After the loss of her child, the murder of her husband, and her affair with Xavier Hawthorne, a ghost, walking away and starting over was her only choice.

When the flight landed, Danielle took a taxi south to Areto, a small town on the west coast filled with a mix of tourists and locals. A hotspot known for its killer waves, every year thousands of people from around the world came for the surf competitions, but most of the time Areto was a laid-back small town far away from the bustle and traffic of the city. She once spent a summer here on one of her mother's misguided adventures.

Danielle checked into a hotel and dumped her suitcase onto the floor. She would have to look for a place to live and a job, but first she needed coffee. She changed into shorts and a tank top. Even at six in the morning, sweat trickled down her forehead. With her pale skin, sunscreen would be necessary before she burned to a crisp.

As she walked down the beach, she noticed huge brown pelicans roosting in the tops of the coconut trees. They occasionally swooped across the sky, gliding with wings as huge as sails, then diving in search of fish. Except for a few more hotels and condos along the shoreline, not much had changed since she had last been here. One of her most vivid childhood memories was of sitting alone on the sand with a notebook, a box of crayons, and a paper bag full of snacks wondering when her mother would come back for her.

Danielle walked up the sandy wooden steps of the Playa Bar. The wood canopy offered a welcome respite from the heat of the sun.

"*Buenos días!*" The girl at the counter smiled as she bustled around the bar to set up for the day, juggling bottles and stacking plates.

"Hi, can I get some coffee and eggs?" Danielle sat on one of the rickety wooden stools that stood on all four sides of the outdoor bar. A large cement patio with now-empty dining tables surrounded the bar and a swimming pool flanked the right side. A hotel was set behind the patio.

"*Sí.* You're up early."

Danielle's high school Spanish consisted of a couple stock phrases, so she was grateful that most of the residents also spoke English.

"Red-eye flight. I just arrived a little while ago." Danielle inhaled the welcome smell of the black coffee as the bartender poured a steaming cup.

"How long are you here for?"

Danielle's heart contracted. *Forever,* she thought. Even that wouldn't be long enough to punish herself for Matt's death.

"I'll be staying indefinitely. Do you know of any places for rent?"

"Actually, I do. Someone just moved out of an apartment my uncle owns. It's down the street from here. It's small, but there's an upstairs apartment and an open space on the first floor. The last tenant had a little shop for souvenirs since it's right on the beach. Are you looking for a job? There's not too much around here."

Danielle doubted she could find work as an art teacher with her limited knowledge of Spanish. She had emptied her bank account when she left, but that would last for only so long.

"I'm not sure what I'm going to do for work, but the apartment sounds perfect. My name's Danielle Williams, by the way."

"I'm Leisa. I'll let my uncle know you're interested. Come back this afternoon and maybe he can show you the apartment."

"That would be great. Thanks, Leisa."

Maybe a bit of luck is finally coming my way, Danielle thought. Leisa's comments about the previous tenant selling souvenirs sparked an idea. Tourists with money in their pockets and piña coladas in their stomachs might be willing to buy anything. Maybe she could paint and sell some of her work.

After breakfast, she crashed in her room for a couple hours, then walked to the corner store to buy supplies, including the desperately needed sunscreen.

On her way back to the Playa Bar that afternoon, she meandered through an obstacle course of people sunning themselves. She envied their carefree joy. She was sure that guilt and pain radiated from her like a plague. The crowd was so wrapped up in their own happiness, she was able to pass through them as if she were invisible. The warm breeze ruffled the soft curls that fell to her shoulders. Danielle typically kept her hair shorter, but for the last four months she had lacked the motivation and energy to get it cut.

In contrast to the calm of this morning, the bar teemed with sandy, sunburned vacationers and pulsed with music. Danielle's pale skin made her stick out as a new arrival. She edged her way into a seat.

"Hey, Danielle, you're back! My uncle will be here soon. Do you want a drink while you're waiting?

"Sure, how about a piña colada, lots of rum."

"Coming right up!" Leisa's long, dark hair swung as she worked and chatted with the other bartenders.

Danielle sipped on her drink and took in the view as the waves rolled and crashed in an unending, hypnotic rhythm.

A boisterous voice next to her interrupted her peaceful reverie.

"*Hola*, Leisa, *qué tal?*"

Danielle glanced out of the corner of her eye. Tan skin, hair bleached blond by the sun and pulled back into a pony-tail, ripped abs. *Definitely a surfer.*

"Hey, Sawyer, *cómo estás?*" Leisa asked as she rang the bell overhead for a generous tip.

"It's all good. Another beautiful day in paradise. Business is good. All these tourists spending their money. The waves look good at the point. A bunch of us are going there later. Want to come?"

"I can't. Maybe another day. My shift doesn't end until five. Hold on, I have to get the phone."

Sawyer leaned his muscled forearms over the bar and turned to Danielle.

"Here on vacation?"

"Not really, I'm staying for a while."

"Hey, Danielle, my uncle asked if he can meet you at the apartment. It's past Sawyer's surf shop. Sawyer, this is Danielle. Danielle, this is Sawyer Reed."

Sawyer's soft, brown eyes sparkled, his hand strong as it gripped hers.

"Nice to meet you. Why don't I walk with you to the apartment? I know right where it is and I'm heading that way."

"No, that's okay. I'm sure I can find it."

"Come on. Think of me as the Areto welcoming committee."

Danielle got the feeling not many people said no to Sawyer. She sucked down the last of her drink and slid off the barstool.

"Good luck with the apartment," Leisa shouted as Danielle followed Sawyer out of the bar.

He practically bounced down the beach. *Maybe some of his happiness will rub off on me*, Danielle thought. *He certainly has plenty to spare.*

"This is my place." Sawyer pointed as they passed a shop with paddleboards and jet skis for rent. The sign above the door advertised scuba diving and surfing lessons. "Do you surf?"

"No, swimming is more my speed. I'm not too coordinated, and me and waves are not a good combination."

"If you change your mind, I can give you a private lesson." Sawyer winked.

"I don't think that's happening, but I'll keep it in mind."

"So how did you end up here?"

Danielle paused for a moment. The real answer was way too much to share. "I wanted a change, that's all."

"Are you always this serious? It's a beautiful day. You're walking next to a handsome guy. What could be better?"

Danielle raised her eyebrows. "It's good to see you're so humble. All I've got is a bunch of sad stories that would completely ruin your island vibe."

"I might have to do something about that. Here we are."

After a short walk, they had arrived at a two-story, square concrete building typical of most of the homes in the area. The porch on the top level opened to the sea. Although the deep blue paint peeled off the walls, Danielle immediately loved it.

A man wearing a crisp, tailored shirt and khaki pants came out front. His leathery, lined face broke into a smile as he extended his hand.

"Hola, you must be Danielle. I'm Ramón. *Mucho gusto.*"

"Nice to meet you too. Thanks for coming to show me the apartment."

"Hola, Sawyer, *qué tal?*" Ramón crushed Sawyer in an enormous bear hug.

"I'm good. I'm on my way back to the shop. The waves and the tourists await." Sawyer reached into his pocket. "Here's one of my cards. In case you ever need anything."

Danielle took the card shoved it in her back pocket.

Sawyer flashed his brilliant smile. "I'll see you around."

"Let me give you a tour of the place. It's small, but it's the best location in town." Ramón unlocked the front door and ushered Danielle into a large room with a counter and shelves on all the walls. Danielle envisioned the shelves filled with her artwork. An open doorway led to a large back room with stairs to the second floor. The top floor consisted of a huge open area that contained a bed, living room area, and a kitchen. A bathroom was tucked in the back corner.

"All the furniture comes with the apartment." The plastic table in the kitchen gave a little crack as Ramón leaned on it. Danielle opened one of the wooden cabinets and a cockroach skittered away. "Those come with the apartment too." Ramón shrugged.

Danielle walked out onto the porch with its breathtaking view of the sea. Cockroaches and all, it was perfect. "I'll take it. How much is it a month?"

"Six hundred dollars for a friend of *mi sobrina* Leisa."

"Can I move in today?"

"Sure, *está bien*. It's empty. It's yours. I'll go get the keys. Do you need a car? There's a beat-up old Mini-Cooper out front. The previous tenant left it when they moved away. The keys are hanging behind the door in the apartment. You're welcome to use it, but drive at your own risk. No registration, but it runs."

Danielle sighed. Maybe this place could be the beginning of her new life.

After paying Ramón, she grabbed the keys to the car and walked outside to the parking lot. He wasn't kidding when he said the car was beat up. Danielle doubted that it ran. Rust holes dotted the car like freckles and a large dent graced the passenger door. When Danielle opened the driver's door, it creaked as if it would fall off the hinges. But to her amazement, when she put the key in the ignition, it started.

By the time she returned from retrieving her suitcase at the hotel and shopping for supplies, the sun blazed and colored the sky a deep red. As the last bit of light dipped into the horizon, customers down the beach at the Playa Bar clapped and cheered. Danielle remembered the daily ritual from her childhood — everyone gathered at the bar to view the beauty of the sunset and applaud as the sun sank into the sea.

Danielle collapsed onto her bed. The sound of the ocean through the open windows did not soothe her. She heard whispers in the wind and water. Ghosts called to her. She wished she could throw her regrets and memories into the waves, but she knew they would only wash up again at her feet like the glittering pieces of sea glass that tumbled onto the sand. Danielle fought to stay awake. She dreaded sleep and the horrors that she knew would invade her dreams.

A light touch on her shoulder woke her. Xavier sat next to her on the bed.

"You're here." Her eyes immediately filled with tears.

"I'll always find you." Xavier strung his fingers through her hair as if it were a delicate strand of pearls.

"But how did you get here? You couldn't leave the house."

"I told you I'd find a way."

Every cell in her body prickled with electricity. She drank in each detail of his beautiful body. Solid as flesh and bone, black hair cascading across his forehead, the wing tattoo curled around his neck. She used to remember his eyes as deep pools where she could drown, but now she saw they were dark coals where she would gladly burn.

Danielle surged forward and embraced him. His arms gripped her with their gentle strength. She felt lost and found at the same moment. His lips pressed against her neck, her hair, and her lips. She kissed him fiercely, wanting to devour him.

"I thought I'd end up alone," Danielle murmured.

"I could never let you go."

Tears spilled down her face. Tears that could erase all the bad memories. Xavier kissed each one away. Her desperate desire for him was a thirst that only he could quench.

She ripped her clothes off and yanked down Xavier's jeans. As he rose above her, she clutched at his muscled shoulders. He entered her slowly and rocked into her. Her entire body quivered with desire. She kept her gaze fixed on Xavier as her body tightened in release. At that moment, Xavier's form wavered and his body slipped through her embrace like water.

Danielle woke, her cheeks wet with tears. Her heart pounded as she curled into a ball. She questioned her decision to leave as violent sobs wracked her body. She knew she loved Xavier, but how could she have any kind of future with a ghost? Above all, she was certain that no matter how far she ran, she would never find peace.

CHAPTER 2

O ver the next several weeks, Danielle tried to settle in to her new life. Her days took on a disjointed rhythm, out of step with the world. It was as if she were made of glass. One false move and her carefully crafted mirage of normalcy would shatter.

Afraid of the dreams that sleep brought, she stayed awake as long as possible. At night, she painted, wandered on the beach, or swam. When she finally succumbed out of exhaustion, she slept until one or two o'clock in the afternoon. She then dragged herself out of bed to open her shop. Danielle did her best to smile and put on a happy mask when people came in. She hoped it would get easier.

This afternoon when Danielle woke up, she immediately regretted falling asleep on the small couch in her studio. Her back and neck ached, stiff from being cramped on the tiny couch. The canvas she had worked on last night towered above her. Wings swirled in a gray mist and dripped with bright red blood. Body parts littered the background. *Definitely not one for the tourists.*

She closed the door to the back room and headed upstairs to slather on some sunscreen and put on her bikini. A swim might do her aching back some good. Downstairs she grabbed her sign advertising Changing Tides Art, a blanket, and a box of her art pieces. During her midnight strolls on the beach, she gathered pieces of driftwood and painted ocean scenes on them. They practically leapt off the shelves.

She arranged the pieces on the blanket, set up her sign, and walked to the water. Entering the ocean felt like slipping into a warm bath, none of the shock that the freezing Northeast held even in the summertime. Because of the large waves, Danielle stayed close to the shore and waded in only to her waist. Although she swam pretty well, she had a healthy respect for the ocean. She peered out at the horizon, ready to sprint back to her towel if a menacing wave rolled in.

"Nice to see you out in daylight hours for once." Sawyer sauntered up next to her.

She had exchanged an occasional wave with him on her way to the Playa Bar for dinner, but other than that, she kept to herself. *Damn.* The sunlight glistened off his tanned skin and taut abs. Women probably hung all over him.

"Yeah, I decided to sell my artwork out here this afternoon."

"That's good because you could use some sun. You are way too pale to live here. So what's with all the late night swims and walks?"

"I didn't know you kept such close tabs on me." Danielle peered across the water.

"You do know that I live right above the surf shop? I sit on my porch at night and look out at the ocean, and there you are."

"I have trouble sleeping." Danielle edged slowly out of the water.

"Where are you going? I'm not stalking you. I didn't mean to creep you out."

"No, it's not that. I'm just avoiding that big wave. I don't feel like drowning today."

Sawyer glanced at the crest forming. "That? Come on now. If you're going to live in Areto, you can't be afraid of the waves. I know you know how to swim. You've got to learn to live a little." He grasped her hand and pulled her deeper.

Danielle tried unsuccessfully to loosen his grip. "Did you happen to notice how short I am? That wave is going to crush me." Danielle eyed the oncoming wave with suspicion.

"Have a little faith, will you?" Sawyer did not let go of her hand. His eyes radiated with the warm, comforting brown of coffee or chocolate. "When I say jump, you jump."

"I don't know. This—"

"Jump!"

Danielle leapt and the wave flowed harmlessly past.

"See?" Sawyer exclaimed with his wide grin. "That wasn't so bad, was it?"

"It was all right, but I'm going to get out now."

"That might not be a good idea." Sawyer squinted at the horizon.

"Why?" Danielle asked. When she turned, she saw an enormous wave rippling toward them. "Let me go!"

"It's too late for that. You'll be right in its path when it breaks. I'll lift you up when it comes." Sayer stepped closer to Danielle and placed both hands on her hips. "Don't worry, I've got you."

He brushed against her, skin to skin. She instinctively pulled away, but as the wave approached, she reached up to grab Sawyer's shoulders.

"Don't you dare drop me."

"I'm a surfer. I am one with the sea. Get ready." The wave barreled closer. "This might be a little bigger than I thought."

Sawyer launched Danielle into the air. She tumbled head over heels until the tide deposited her on the sand. Sawyer's legs appeared in front of her as she caught her breath.

"What happened to 'don't worry I've got you'?" Danielle spluttered.

"Sorry about that. You might want to fix your, uh, …" Sawyer gestured to her chest.

Danielle glanced down. In the tumult, the strap of her top had come undone, revealing one of her breasts.

"Do you need help?" Sawyer chuckled.

"No, you've helped quite enough for today." Danielle quickly pulled it up and retied the strap.

"I'll make it up to you. A drink at the Playa later?" He reached down to help her stand.

"I don't think so." Danielle brushed the sand off her legs, her cheeks flushed.

"One of these days, you and I are going to have some fun." Sawyer grinned as he strolled down the beach toward the surf shop.

When the beach began to empty, Danielle packed up.

After showering, she rescued her tarot deck from the jumble of blankets on her bed and sat on her porch to eat. She shuffled the cards and pulled out the Hermit. *How appropriate. That's what I'll become, a lonely old hermit living my life alone by the sea. All I need is a cat.*

Danielle's phone buzzed.

"Hi, Karen!"

"How are you doing? Did you settle into your new place yet?" Danielle wouldn't have survived without her best friend Karen. Danielle had been in a haze right after Matt's murder, and Karen took over, even having Danielle move in with her and her husband Brian. She had texted Karen to let her know where she'd gone, but they hadn't spoken since the day she left.

"Yeah, things are going okay."

"Only you would describe living in the Caribbean as okay when we're freezing our asses off up here in Fairview. I'm glad you're settled because I'm making plans to come visit you."

"It would be great to have company. Is Brian coming too?"

"No, it'll just be me. Brian can't take time off from work, but I am looking forward to having my ass in the sand, a drink in my hand, and some hot guys for my viewing pleasure."

"I'll see what I can do. Text me with the details and I'll pick you up at the airport."

"I will. Take care and I'll see you soon."

Danielle hung up and shuffled her tarot deck again. This time she pulled out the Knight of Wands, on his horse in his shiny armor ready to save the fair maiden. Danielle's mind drifted back to Sawyer and his strong arms lifting her above the waves. She shook her head to erase the image.

She didn't believe in fairy tales or happy endings anymore. No prince would come to rescue her from her dark dreams.

After dinner, Danielle went to her studio. Engrossed in her painting, the knock on her studio door startled her.

"Whoa, you're a little jumpy." Sawyer strolled into the back room. "I came to take you for that drink I promised you earlier today." He had traded in his swim trunks for khaki shorts and a pale pink, collared shirt. His blond hair flowed loosely on his shoulders.

"I'm going to stay in and keep working. I'm kind of on a roll."

"Are you sure? It'll be a good time. You can't stay holed up in your apartment forever, you know."

"I'm really not in the mood for a party right now. And I sold quite a bit today, so I need to replenish my inventory." A bar filled with deliriously happy drunk people was the last place she could picture herself right now.

"Your paintings are really good, by the way. Would you be interested in doing a mural on one of the walls of the surf shop, maybe an ocean scene? Nothing like that." Sawyer pointed to the large canvas teeming with wings, blood, eyes, and tangled limbs. "You might scare the tourists away with that one."

Danielle quickly threw a sheet over the canvas. "I don't know about a mural. I've never done anything on that scale before."

"Come on. I'm sure you can use the money and I've been thinking about painting the outside forever. Please say yes."

"I'll think about it."

"Great! Come by whenever you want. You know where to find me. And if you change your mind about that drink, walk down to the bar."

The screen door slammed behind Sawyer as he left. Danielle uncovered her painting. She traced her hand over the wing, the entwined arms, and the dark eyes. She thought back to the picture she sketched the last night she and Xavier had spent together — Xavier's face with her green eyes reflected in his. She wondered if it lay crumpled on the floor of the house gathering dust. Danielle threw the sheet back over the painting and returned to her work. She felt like a fraud sketching tranquil beach scenes when inside her, chaos and shadows reigned.

Around eleven, hoping to put off sleep for as long as she could, she put her brushes in to soak, closed her paints, and decided to go for a swim. The crash of the surf muffled the noise and music from the bar. She slipped into the warm water and floated on her back. She enjoyed the solitude of the ocean at night and relaxed into the gentle sway and hush of the waves. The stars blazed above her. She wondered if Xavier looked out the window at the same sky.

When she finally got out, she shivered and wished she had brought a towel. Clouds crept in and devoured the stars, making it difficult to pick her way up the beach. She was concentrating so hard, she stumbled into a woman who sat crossed-legged in the sand.

"*Lo siento*! I didn't see you there." Danielle skirted around her.

The woman called back. "*Está bien, mija*. Haven't you heard the stories?"

"The stories? I'm sorry, I'm not sure what you mean."

"They say that ghosts haunt the seas at night. You swim at night, you swim with the spirits. I'm Vanessa, by the way. My place is next to the Wave Hotel. Come by. I can read your palm or tell your future." Vanessa rose. Tall and thin, her straight, dark hair reached her waist.

"Thanks for the offer, but I'd rather keep my future a mystery."

"Why be afraid of your future? It's going to happen one way or another. But do be careful. We don't want to lose you to the spirits." Her long skirt and hair whipped in the wind as she walked away.

That was a little creepy, thought Danielle. She closed the apartment door and trudged upstairs dreading the dreams that would trespass through her sleep.

CHAPTER 3

anielle finally worked up the courage to paint the mural. When she arrived at the surf shop, a group of bikini-clad women gathered around Sawyer while they waited for paddleboards. They practically drooled all over him and hung on every one of his words. No wonder Sawyer's business was so successful. One of them giggled and leaned forward to touch his chest. Danielle didn't blame her. He had a gorgeous body. She imagined he used it to his advantage whenever possible. Sawyer caught her eye, and she waited while he set the women up on their paddleboards. He walked up to her with a wide grin.

"Good to see you out in the sun again. We might make a beach bum out of you yet."

"It's possible, I guess. Can you show me where you want the mural?"

"Right here on this wall." Sawyer showed her the side of the building. "People who walk by will be able to see it, right? Just remember, peaceful beach scene, none of that dark, blood-and-death stuff you do on the side."

"Got it." Danielle smiled. "And how much will you pay me for this one of a kind masterpiece of happiness that I'll be creating?"

"Does $800 sound fair?"

"I'll do it."

"Beautiful! We're kind of busy right now. I'll be out front if you need anything. Come over whenever you have time."

Danielle measured the wall, and evaluated the surface. The concrete was in pretty good shape, but it would require a coat of primer. Danielle took out her sketchpad to draw a scale model and hoped she hadn't gotten in over her head.

She returned the next day to start painting. Once in a while, people gathered behind her to watch. At first, Danielle was so self-conscious she could barely make a mark, used to the solitude of her studio. As time passed, she grew accustomed to working in a fishbowl. She should have made business cards to hand out, but she just pointed to her shop and hoped it would lead to some sales.

Danielle assessed her progress, happy with how she had captured the shifting blues and greens of the ocean. Backing up for a better perspective, Danielle jumped when she collided with Sawyer who stood a few steps behind her.

"How long have you been there? You're awfully quiet, sneaking up on people."

"I was watching you paint. Admiring the view...the view of the picture, that is." Sawyer smirked. "Relax. You're about to leap out of your skin."

"That's what happens when people sneak up on you and don't announce their presence."

"Geez, are you an artist or an English teacher? But I will be sure to 'announce my presence' in the future. I'm going upstairs to grab lunch. Why don't you come with me?"

Danielle hesitated, but agreed. At the mere mention of food, her stomach growled.

Stairs at the back of the shop led to an apartment similar to hers with a wrap-around porch. Danielle expected a sloppy bachelor pad, but instead, a cozy interior decorated with warm blues and grays greeted her. Even his bed was made, in contrast to hers, which resembled a nest. Books, sketchpads, and pencils were tucked inside a mass of tangled sheets back at her place. His apartment was definitely a step up from her cockroach-infested one with its plastic table and chairs. She was even more surprised to find an entire wall lined with bookshelves.

"Who's the English teacher?" Danielle asked as she ran her fingers across the titles on the shelf: Dante, Shakespeare, Yeats, Poe. "Did you really read all these or is this just a clever ruse to impress the girls you bring here?"

"Of course I've read them. I'm hurt. Did you think I was just a dumb surfer?"

"Yeah, kind of."

"Did my ruse work? Are you impressed?"

"I need a little more than that to be impressed. Quote me a line from one of these books and maybe I'll change my mind."

Sawyer cradled her hands in his, and gazed into her eyes.

"Shall I compare thee to a summer's day?

Thou art more lovely and more temperate.

Rough winds do shake the darling buds of May,
And summer's lease hath all too short a date.
Sometime too hot the eye of heaven shines,
And often is his gold complexion dimmed;
And every fair from fair sometimes declines,
By chance, or nature's changing course, untrimmed;
But thy eternal summer shall not fade,
Nor lose possession of that fair thou ow'st,
Nor shall death brag thou wand'rest in his shade,
When in eternal lines to Time thou grow'st.
So long as men can breathe, or eyes can see,
So long lives this, and this gives life to thee. "

When he finished, Sawyer lifted his brows. "Impressed?"

Danielle pulled her hands away and gave him a little shove. "No," she laughed. "You probably memorized that just to lure unsuspecting women into your bed. Shakespeare, very cliché."

"You've caught on to my evil plan. But just so you know, I was pre-law at Columbia before I decided to ditch it all for this." Sawyer gestured at the beautiful view outside the window. "Nearly gave my parents a heart attack when I dropped out, but here I am."

"That's something we have in common. I am an eternal disappointment to my mother."

"I knew we had a deep cosmic connection. Let's get some lunch."

After Sawyer made sandwiches, they ate on the porch and watched people pass by. He chattered away happily and shared funny stories about the tourists he'd met through his surf shop.

Danielle appreciated the fact that Sawyer never asked her about her past. He spared her any annoying or painful personal questions. A little bit of darkness lurked in every-one, but so far Sawyer seemed as fluffy, white, and buoyant as a cloud in the blue sky.

The mural was almost finished. The last step would be to add a sealant. Done painting for the day, Danielle went to the Playa Bar for lunch while Sawyer surfed at the Point.

"Hi, Danielle! Haven't seen you around lately." Leisa hustled behind the bar as she mixed drinks and prepared food.

"I've been painting the mural over at the surf shop."

"I noticed you've been over there a lot. Are you sure it's only about the mural?" Leisa winked.

"Absolutely. Business, that's all. Maybe we're friends, I guess."

"Business? Friends? I think you're a little confused yourself."

"I'm really not interested in a relationship right now."

"If you say so."

Danielle ordered *pinchos* and *tostones*. As she ate her lunch, the woman from the other night, Vanessa, passed by.

"Do you see that woman walking by?" Danielle questioned Leisa.

"Yeah, that's Vanessa Rivera. She's a medium, psychic, whatever you call it. She's a bit *loca*, if you know what I mean. She does these group readings at the hotel. You should go. It's a little weird, but entertaining."

"My friend Karen is coming for a visit this Friday. Maybe we'll go. I met Vanessa the other night on the beach. She told me spirits roamed the ocean at night."

"That's an old superstition. Do you swim at night?"

"Yeah, when I can't sleep."

"I wouldn't be worried about ghosts, but there's other stuff out there—sharks, rip currents. *Ten cuidado, chica.*"

At that moment, Sawyer entered the bar accompanied by a gorgeous woman with the biggest breasts Danielle had ever seen. She wondered how they stayed captive in her skimpy bikini, and how she managed to balance on a surfboard with all that counterweight.

Sawyer whispered in her ear. She smiled and strolled over to a table.

"Hey, Leisa, Danielle. *Dos cervezas, por favor.*"

"I thought you were surfing all day today," Danielle said.

"Change of plans."

"I finished the mural today. I just need to put the sealant on top. Take a look later and tell me what you think."

Sawyer's face flickered with concern for an instant before it returned to his usual carefree expression.

"I'll stop by later with the money."

"No rush, you know where to find me."

"I was getting used to having you around. Who am I going to eat lunch with now?"

"I don't think that will be a problem."

The woman at the table blew a kiss at Sawyer.

"Just don't be a stranger." He leaned forward and rubbed his thumb against her jawline to remove a blob of blue paint.

Danielle imagined how it would feel to be touched other places by his strong, callused hands.

"You didn't flinch this time. Progress, we're making progress. Thanks for the beers, Leisa. See you later."

Leisa raised her eyebrows. "Friends, huh?"

CHAPTER 4

On Friday morning, Danielle drove to Aguadilla to pick up Karen from the airport. She scanned the crowd as people exited the terminal. As soon as she saw Karen, she broke into a smile. A piece of home had arrived. Since they'd met, Karen had always taken care of her. She was more of a mother to her than her biological one.

Karen rushed over to her, dropped her suitcase, and gave Danielle a huge hug. "It's so good to see you. You're so tan and your hair's growing out. You actually look like you live on the beach!"

"I've missed you!" Danielle hugged her friend, then immediately pulled away. "Something's wrong. What's wrong?" Karen shifted nervously from foot to foot. "Is it Brian? Is he okay?"

"I'm really sorry. I was going to tell you, but she made me promise and you know how she is."

Danielle's jaw dropped and she shook her head. "No, no, please tell me she's not here." Danielle searched the passengers. Marla Parker, her mother, waved. Danielle managed a weak smile as she muttered to Karen, "I'm going to kill you, you do know that."

Karen shrugged and mouthed *sorry* as Marla headed towards Danielle.

"Are you surprised? When I heard Karen was coming here, I wanted to surprise you!"

Danielle had a rocky relationship with her mother. Marla lacked any warm, nurturing qualities. She firmly believed that her job as a mother was to let her child figure out everything on her own. Her priority had been to make Danielle independent, and her method to achieve this goal consisted of benign neglect.

Danielle gave her mother an obligatory hug. Marla's short, spiky hair was white with green tips. A new piercing graced her nose.

"How long are you planning to stay?"

"Until Monday, like Karen," Marla squeezed Danielle's cheeks. "Your hair's longer. I like it. But you're very pale and those bags under your eyes… You look like you could use some sleep."

"I know your apartment is small, so I made a reservation at a hotel. Your mom can stay with you." Karen gave Danielle a sheepish grin.

"Great, that's great. Thanks, Karen." Danielle glared at her friend. "I'll sleep in my studio and you can sleep upstairs, Mom."

"Let's go, people! There's a drink and a spot on the sand with my name on it. And hopefully, some gorgeous men parading by." Karen dragged Danielle off. They shoved their bags and themselves into Danielle's tiny car for the twenty-minute drive back to Areto.

Danielle dropped Karen off at her hotel and waited while she changed into her bathing suit. Then they continued on to Danielle's apartment where Danielle and her mother got ready.

After they settled themselves on the beach, Danielle and Karen walked to the bar to get drinks while Marla soaked up the sun in her beach chair.

"I'm never going to forgive you for this," Danielle said.

"You're my best friend, you have to forgive me. She's your mother. What could I do? It'll still be fun."

"Hi, Leisa, could we get three piña coladas? This is my friend Karen. My mom's here too."

"Nice to meet you, Karen. You know Vanessa's giving a reading at the hotel next door tonight at 8:00. You should go."

"We'll think about it. I'm sure we'll be back for more drinks. With my mother here, alcohol will be mandatory."

"No worries, there's an endless supply," Leisa laughed.

Danielle and Karen brought the drinks back to their chairs.

"Now this is the life." Karen stretched out and sipped on her piña colada.

The ocean rippled with soft waves. The blue sky seemed to reach on forever. Because of the calm seas, paddleboarders and kayakers dominated the water. Sawyer waved at Danielle as he helped some people into a kayak.

"He's super-hot. Who's that?" Karen exclaimed.

"That's Sawyer, a friend. I painted the mural on his surf shop." Danielle gestured at the wall behind them.

"It's beautiful, Danielle! I always thought that you should paint. That teaching stuff wasted your talent," Marla said.

"I might need a private paddleboarding lesson from Sawyer," Karen sighed. "Look at that body. And he's heading straight for us."

Danielle agreed. Sawyer was hot. His blond hair, usually back in a ponytail, shook loose on his shoulders. He sauntered up like an Adonis or a model on the cover of a cheesy romance novel in the supermarket.

"Hi, Danielle. You must introduce me to these lovely ladies."

"This is my friend, Karen, and my mom, Marla. This is Sawyer."

"It's a beautiful day for paddleboarding. Are you guys interested?" Sawyer asked. "On the house, of course."

"We're good enjoying our drinks and the sun." Danielle leaned back in her chair and put on her sunglasses.

"Oh no, I'm here. I want the full experience and you're coming with me!" Karen exclaimed.

"That's the spirit!" Sawyer said. "How about you, Marla?"

"I spent the last six months on a boat off the coast of Alaska. I'm staying right here on land. But you two go ahead."

"Great! Finish your drinks and I'll go get two boards and meet you down by the water."

Karen watched Sawyer walk back to the shop. "Oh my God, do you see how he looks at you, Danielle? If you don't fuck that boy, I might."

"Karen!" Danielle shouted.

"I agree with Karen. A good one-night stand can be very liberating." Marla pulled down her sunglasses to get a long look at Sawyer.

And you're an expert on that, she thought. When Danielle was twelve, Marla told her that she was the product of a one-night stand. Her father probably didn't even know she existed. Danielle doubted her mother even knew for certain who he was.

"It's probably my fault," Marla continued. "You were always searching for the father you never had growing up, looking for someone to take care of you. Not to speak ill of the dead, but Matt wasn't right for you. He came into your life and took over. You never explored your sexual independence."

"Thanks for the mini psychoanalysis, Mom, appreciate it."

Karen and Danielle sucked down the last of their drinks.

Sawyer met them on the shore with two paddleboards. "I'm going to give you a little lesson before you go out there so you know what you're doing. First, you're going to strap this cord to your ankle, so if you fall off you don't lose your board."

"Great, we're already talking about falling off. Don't we need to wear life jackets?" Danielle asked.

Sawyer put his hand on Danielle's shoulder. "No, no lifejackets, this is the Wild West. Besides, you're not going to fall. And if you do, you're a good swimmer. Just climb back on the board. You're perfect for this, low center of gravity and all."

"Short, you mean I'm short." Danielle scowled.

"Well...yes."

"What's next?" Karen asked.

"Hop on the board. You should start out kneeling and then slowly get up one leg at a time. Stand in the middle of the board, your feet about shoulder distance apart." Sawyer stood behind Danielle and placed his hands on her hips. "Spread your legs a little farther apart. That's good. Remember to keep your core tight. That's what's going to keep your balance." Sawyer centered one hand on her stomach to illustrate his point.

His hand on her bare skin caused a tingling sensation to course down Danielle's belly. She turned her head to Karen who mouthed, *OMG!*

Sawyer continued. "Grab your paddles. You're going to use both hands when you stroke."

Karen snickered. Danielle didn't dare look at her as she picked up her paddle.

"No, not that way. Your right hand should be on top of the shaft. Your left hand in the middle, and then take long, deep pulls." Sawyer hands curved over Danielle's as they moved together practicing with the paddle.

Sawyer's warm skin grazed against her back, his arms around her. It felt very intimate as he slid his hands up the length of her arms to her shoulders. Danielle trembled under his touch. "Are you guys ready? Any questions?"

"Oh, we're ready. You got us all primed." Karen grinned from ear to ear.

"Then get out there!"

Danielle and Karen pushed their boards into the surf. After a few shaky attempts, both were able to stand.

"If Sawyer didn't stop talking about shafts and stroking, I could have had an orgasm right on that board. How did you stand it with him behind you with his hands on you? He definitely likes you."

"No he doesn't. He has a million girls all over him."

"And you could be a million and one. I bet he's got a huge dick. Did you feel it when he stood behind you? Was he hard?"

"I'd smack you with this paddle but I'd fall off the board. No, I did not feel his dick!"

"But you should! Like he said, one hand on the top of the shaft, the other in the middle, and take long, deep pulls,"

Karen mimicked Sawyer's voice. "I'm telling you right now, you and that boy are going to get it on."

Danielle laughed. It felt good to have her friend with her. With Karen, she could almost pretend she was one of the happy people on vacation here. Danielle enjoyed skimming peacefully over the top of the waves, and was surprised at how easy it was.

When they returned to shore, Sawyer waited for them.

"I didn't see either of you fall out there. How was it?"

"We had a great time," Danielle said. "How much do these boards cost?"

"See, your beach bum status keeps creeping forward! The good ones cost about $800. We could do a trade. A board in exchange for the mural?"

"That sounds good." Danielle pictured herself out on the paddleboard at night under the stars.

"Come on. Let's take a look at what's in the shop."

After perusing the boards available, Danielle picked out one with a purple lotus flower.

They spent the rest of the afternoon sunning themselves on the beach while Karen filled them in on the latest gossip in Fairview.

After dinner, they walked to the hotel for the psychic reading. Karen and Marla chatted away, but an anxious knot twisted in Danielle's stomach. She didn't have a great track record when it came to mediums or psychics.

Outside the large conference room, a sign read, Vanessa Rivera: Medium, Messages from Beyond. About thirty chairs filled the room. Danielle, Karen, and Marla sat in the middle row.

By 7:00, the room was nearly full. Vanessa appeared wearing a long, flowing black skirt and a tank top. Tonight her hair was pulled back in a severe ponytail. Tattoos of roses, skulls, and crosses covered her arms and chest.

"Welcome," said Vanessa. "You all came tonight because you wish to hear from a loved one who has passed. Spirit does what spirit wants, so I can't guarantee who will come through or even that you'll be read."

Danielle squirmed in her chair. She didn't know what she wished for. She wasn't sure if she would be able to handle hearing from anyone — her daughter, Matt, or Xavier for that matter.

Vanessa continued. "Spirit will speak through me, and sometimes act through me. If I have a message for you, please say yes if it makes sense to you or you understand. There are strong spirits here with us tonight. Let's get started."

Danielle breathed in the sadness in the room. So many people who longed to connect with their lost ones. A couple of times, Vanessa stepped toward Danielle, but then turned and approached another person. Toward the end of the night, Danielle was relieved that it was almost over. It drained her to listen to all the sorrowful stories. Karen checked her watch, and after traveling and a long day in the sun, Marla started to snore.

A strong gust of wind blew into the room and slammed the door shut. Danielle, along with most of the people in the room, jumped. Vanessa closed her eyes and her body quivered. She shook her arms, then ran her hands down her neck and over her chest. Karen gave Danielle a quizzical look. Danielle shrugged, but the knot in her stomach rose.

Vanessa opened her eyes and stared at her. "Danielle?" she inquired.

"Yes," Danielle replied weakly.

Vanessa walked over and knelt in front of her so that they were eye to eye. "I have a wing tattoo. Do you understand this?"

Danielle's heart pounded wildly as she nodded.

"I'm here. I'm searching, always searching for you. I will find a way back to you. Don't give up on me."

Danielle closed her eyes and took a deep breath.

Vanessa ran a hand through Danielle's hair and down the side of her cheek. She leaned forward and kissed Danielle on the lips. "I'll never leave you, Danielle."

Xavier's face flashed in her mind. Unthinking, she grabbed Vanessa and returned her kiss.

Abruptly, Vanessa jerked back and pushed away from Danielle. Marla and Karen's mouths gaped open. Vanessa steadied herself, and then wandered back to the front of the room.

"Spirit manifested with strength tonight. That's all for this session. My cards are on the table if anyone wants to schedule a private reading. Be well and remember, you are loved even from beyond."

As everyone filed out, Danielle turned to look back at Vanessa. Her forehead creased and she stared at Danielle as if she were trying to see into her soul. People whispered and giggled at Danielle as they walked past.

Karen clutched Danielle's arm and pulled her out of the room. "What the fuck, Danielle! She kissed you and you kissed her back! What was all that about? A wing tattoo? Did Matt have a wing tattoo?"

"Did you like the kiss, dear? I once had a fling with a girl in college. Phoebe was her name. I haven't thought about her in ages."

"Oh, my God, Mom. Stop, just stop. Too much information. No, Matt didn't have a tattoo."

"Then who was it? Who was she talking about? Who has a wing tattoo?" Karen prattled on.

Danielle gulped. As much as she trusted Karen, she'd never told her about Xavier. The story seemed too crazy for even her best friend to believe.

"I know!" Karen exclaimed. "Xavier Hawthorne who owned your house before you. He had a wing tattoo. Are you being haunted by Xavier Hawthorne?"

"Don't be ridiculous," said Marla. "These people are professionals. They probably look us all up on Facebook or Google or whatever and find out all about us. Are you okay? You look a little pale, Danielle."

"She's in shock. It's not every day you get kissed by a medium. It certainly made for an interesting end to the evening."

After saying goodnight to Karen, Danielle and Marla walked back to the apartment. Danielle settled her mother upstairs, then went to her studio. Tonight she wished for sleep, hoping that Xavier would visit her dreams. She ran a thumb over her lips. Vanessa's kiss had stirred up the longing for Xavier that always simmered below the surface of her consciousness.

After spending the next day enjoying the sun and the beach, they were ready for a night out at the Playa Bar. A salsa band played on Saturday nights, so a big crowd would be there. Danielle hadn't been to the bar at night yet, but being around Karen pushed her out of her comfort zone. She picked out a black, backless, strappy sundress to wear that showed off her newly tanned skin. Her hair, bleached by the sun, made her green eyes stand out even more. As she brushed on lip gloss, she remembered Vanessa's kiss from last night. She wondered if she would ever feel Xavier's kiss again.

Before she left, Danielle shuffled her tarot deck. She split the cards and turned over the top one. The Knight of Wands. *That damn card again. I do not want to be saved.* She shouted upstairs, "Ready to go?"

"All set. I'm ready for a night of dancing!"

"Really, Mom? Nice outfit." Marla wore a glittery sequined top and a short skirt. Her enormous hoop earrings jangled as she came down the stairs.

"Honestly, Danielle, I don't know how you can be my daughter. You're so uptight. Let's go."

A crowd already danced to the band that jammed in the corner of the bar. The beat of the music pulsed through the floor. Karen had gotten an early start and sat at the bar sipping on a drink in an enormous coconut.

"Hey, guys, you're here!"

"What is that?" Marla eyed Karen's drink with longing. "I want one of those."

"Some coconut rum concoction. It's delicious."

Leisa came over to take their order. "What's up, ladies?"

"We'll take two of the coconut drink that she has." Marla pointed to Karen.

"It's going to be one of those nights, is it?" Leisa smiled. "Be careful. Those drinks are strong."

All of a sudden Sawyer was behind Danielle, his hands on her shoulders. He whispered in her ear. "I heard you kissed a girl last night. Did you like it?"

Danielle turned to Sawyer. "No, it wasn't... It wasn't her. It was…oh never mind."

"Mmm hmm, I wish I had been there to see it." Sawyer winked. "You ladies have a good time tonight." He returned to his table at the back of the bar. The girl from the other day sat next to him.

"He is so hot for you." Karen twirled her straw in her drink.

"Did you see where he's sitting? With that gorgeous surfer girl?"

"Yeah, but I also see him looking over here at you."

Sawyer waved at Danielle, and she quickly turned away.

Saving her from continuing this conversation, Leisa's uncle Ramón appeared at the bar. "Hola, how's the apartment working out for you Danielle?"

"It's been great. Ramón, this is my friend Karen and my mom Marla."

"*Encantado*, Marla. A beautiful name for a beautiful woman. Do you know how to dance salsa?"

"I don't, but I'm sure you can teach me."

"Of course, of course. Let's go. *A bailar!*" Ramón grabbed Marla's hand and led her to the dance floor.

"Your mom sure knows how to party," Karen laughed.

Danielle shook her head. The rest of the night they drank, shot pool, and Karen even managed to drag Danielle out on the dance floor. After midnight, Karen yawned. "I'm going to head back to my room. Early flight back and all tomorrow."

"I'm going to be so sad when you leave. It was really good to see you." Danielle hugged her friend.

"Please take care of yourself. I'll definitely come back to visit, and you know you can always move home. Although I don't know why you would want to leave this."

"Thanks. I'll pick you up in the morning. I'm going to stay a little longer to make sure my mom makes it back to the apartment."

After Karen left, Danielle sat at the bar and sipped on her drink. Tired and tipsy, she wished she could go home. She glanced over at the dance floor where Sawyer wrapped his arms around his date. Her mother left Ramón and headed her way. *Thank God. I can finally leave and get in bed.*

"Darling, can I get the key to the apartment?" Marla pulled a compact from her bag and fluffed her hair.

"Why do you need the key? I'll walk back with you."

"Ramón and I are going back to the apartment…for a drink."

"You're kidding, right?"

"What, we're two adults. We're allowed to have fun too, you know. Just give me the key." Danielle grudgingly handed it over. "See you later, sweetheart. I'll leave the door unlocked for you."

As Marla left arm in arm with Ramón, Danielle groaned.

"Do you want another drink?" Leisa asked.

"Yes, give me another one of those coconut things. Looks like I'm going to be here for a while. Did you notice who left together?"

"Sí, your mom and Ramón."

Danielle considered barging in on Karen and sleeping in her room tonight, but figured that Karen was already out cold. She would stay here until the coast was clear. Passing out on the bar seemed to be a better option than going home and listening to her mother get it on above her. Danielle slugged back her drink. The alcoholic buzz did nothing to dull her annoyance. She rested her forehead on the bar and wished for a place to curl up and go to sleep.

"Are you passed out?" Sawyer slid into the seat next to her.

"Not yet," Danielle mumbled.

"Two glasses of water, Leisa. One for me and one for this slug lying on your bar."

Danielle lifted her head. "Slug? Shouldn't you be over there with your girlfriend?"

"I'm only trying to help. Did everyone abandon you?"

"My friend is probably sleeping on a comfy bed and my mom is in the process of fucking Leisa's uncle. Did I say that out loud? Maybe I do need that water."

"Go, mom!" Sawyer pumped his fist in the air. "Good for her!"

"Ugghh. No, no, not good."

"I have a couch you can crash on."

"Yeah, I'm sure Malibu Barbie over there would really appreciate that."

"Desireé? She's not my girlfriend, by the way. She's a great surfer, but kind of a ditz."

"So you like ditzy women?"

"Not exactly."

"Then what is it? It must be big boobs. You like women with big boobs?"

"You are drunk. I like you and well…you know what they say. More than a mouthful is a waste."

"Isn't the expression more than a handful?"

"Mouth, hand — we all have our preferences," Sawyer countered.

This conversation was headed in the wrong direction. Danielle slipped off the bar stool and took a few unsteady steps. "I'm going to walk home. They're old, they're probably done by now. Can you please point me in the right direction?"

"I'm coming with you. You might end up in the ocean at the rate you're going. Give me a second."

Against her better judgement, Danielle waited for him to return.

"Let's go, you drunk." Sawyer grabbed her hand and led her out of the bar.

After a couple minutes of walking in the sand, Danielle's feet felt like they were filled with cement. The ground tipped at a precarious angle.

"It's too far. I need to sit and rest." Danielle slumped on the sand.

"You are a pathetic drunk." Sawyer peered down at her.

"You're full of compliments tonight. Slug, flat-chested, pathetic. But yes, right now, I am a pathetic drunk."

Sawyer chuckled. "Up you go." He pulled her to her feet and threw her over his shoulder, one arm wrapped underneath her dress across her legs, the other hand on her ass steadying her. "My shop is just a little farther. You're sleeping on the couch tonight."

Danielle lacked the energy to protest. He carried her to his apartment, dropped her on the couch, and collapsed next to her. "Whew, you made me work up a sweat. That was like carrying a sack of cement."

Danielle shoved his arm.

"I see it's not your charming wit that wins over the girls."

"No, it's usually the hair." Sawyer pulled out his ponytail and shook his long locks in Danielle's face.

"That's what they go for?"

"And then there's always this." Sawyer pulled his shirt over his head and pointed to his abs. "Come on, who could resist this?"

Danielle burst out in hysterics.

"It's good to hear you laugh even if you are drunk out of your mind."

"Is this the point where you start to recite poetry?"

He leaned closer and tucked a strand of her hair behind her ear.

"'She walks in beauty, like the night
Of cloudless climes and starry skies
And all that's best of dark and bright
Meet in her aspect and her eyes.
Your eyes are so beautiful Danielle, green like the sea."

"Lord Byron, nice. My mom and Karen said I should just get it over with and fuck you." Danielle cringed. The combination of alcohol and hot guy severely impaired her verbal filter.

"You should always listen to your mother, but I'd at least want you to remember it." Sawyer abruptly stood up and threw her a blanket from the bed. "Try to get some sleep. I'll wake you before I go to work."

Danielle curled up on the couch and wrapped the blanket over her head in embarrassment. She fell asleep to the rhythmic song of the coquí frog drifting on the breeze.

Danielle woke as the first rays of sunlight crept through the open windows. The smell of coffee wafted through the apartment. She sat up, now sober but with a throbbing head and a stomach filled with rolling waves. Through the open door of the porch, she saw Sawyer swung in a hammock as he sipped on a cup of coffee.

She tiptoed into the bathroom and closed the door. One look in the mirror and she wished she could make a quick escape, but she knew it would be rude not to at least say goodbye. She did her best to tame her unruly curls, then splashed water on her face. Smears of mascara spread down the inner corners of her eyes, making her look like a rabid raccoon. She grabbed the toothpaste from the side of the sink and squeezed some on her finger, doing her best to rid her mouth of the stale taste of alcohol.

When she finished her clean-up triage, she walked out onto the porch.

"Look who's up." Sawyer patted the hammock and slid over to make room.

"Thanks for the couch last night."

As Danielle sat down, Sawyer threw his arm over her shoulder. Danielle instinctively shrank as if she could shield herself from his touch. They rocked in silence, watching the sky slowly unfold with the pink brushstrokes of dawn.

"Why do you always do that?" An uncharacteristically serious look crossed Sawyer's face.

"Do what?"

"Pull away every time I get close to you. We're friends, right?"

"Yeah, it's just...there's someone else."

"And this someone else. Is he here?"

"No," Danielle sighed.

"Is he coming here?"

"No."

"Then I think he's irrelevant at the moment." Sawyer turned and traced his hand down Danielle's arm, causing a tingling in her belly.

"We hardly know each other."

"Come on, we've eaten lunch together for weeks. I saved you from a rogue wave, taught you to paddleboard. I'd say that counts."

Danielle tried to think of something to say before things got carried away. "Tell me something no one else knows about you."

Sawyer paused for a moment. "I sing Barry Manilow songs in the shower. "Copacabana" is a personal favorite. Now your turn. What's your deep, dark secret?"

"I see ghosts and sometimes things in my dreams are real," Danielle blurted.

"Ghosts, huh? I always knew you were a little twisted." Sawyer smiled. "So that's settled. We're practically soul mates now." Sawyer bent closer and kissed her. His soft lips tasted salty. He pulled back, questioning. Danielle's stomach did flip-flops. *Nerves*, she thought. Then all of a sudden she knew it wasn't nerves. She was going to throw up. She pushed him away and stood shakily. "I've got to go. I don't feel good. I'm sorry."

"Danielle—"

Danielle didn't wait to hear the rest of his sentence. She bolted from the apartment and flew down the stairs. The door slammed behind her. *Please, please don't follow me.* She ran, knowing she had moments before her stomach forcibly rejected all the rum she'd consumed last night. Danielle reached the edge of the surf in time to retch into the water.

"Are you okay?" Sawyer touched her back tentatively.

"Go away please. This is embarrassing enough."

"Oh come on. You're not the first girl I've seen throw up. Maybe the first to throw up right after I've kissed her. That was a real blow to my manhood."

"Just go, please."

"No way. I'm like the chivalrous knight who must return the fair maiden to her castle."

"What did you say?"

"You know, like Prince Charming."

Danielle thought back to the Knight of Wands that she continued to pull from the tarot deck. A shiver coursed down her spine that had nothing to do with the dry heaves that wracked her body.

"Let me walk you home. But warn me if you're going to vomit. I might be chivalrous, but I'm not a martyr."

Danielle and Sawyer walked slowly back to her apartment. Luckily, her mother hadn't locked the door.

"Thanks, Sawyer."

"And I bid you farewell." He kissed the top of her head.

Inside, Danielle checked the clock. It was already time to leave for the airport. As she started upstairs to wake her mom, one of the lizards that frequented her building skittered out of the way as Ramón descended.

"Good morning, Danielle. Have a great day!" Ramón exited hurriedly out the front door.

Up in the apartment, Marla leaned over her suitcase trying to close the zipper. "Good morning, darling, how are you?"

"Hung over, and you?"

"Fabulous! There's nothing like a Latin lover, you know. You never could hold your alcohol."

Danielle held her head to stop the pounding. "Just meet me in the car when you're done packing. We need to leave soon and I wouldn't want you to miss your flight."

When her mom finished packing, they picked up Karen at her hotel and began the drive to the airport.

"Those drinks did me in. I passed out when I got back to my room. Did you stay much later?" Karen asked Danielle.

"Long enough to get sufficiently wasted."

"Oh no! You're such a lightweight. Did you make it home all right?"

"Yeah, I crashed on Sawyer's couch and then he walked me back to the apartment."

"He did. Oh my God. Did you guys do it? Details please!"

"He kissed me and then I ran off and vomited. I'm pretty sure that's never going to happen."

"You didn't!"

"Unfortunately, yes I did."

Marla patted Danielle's arm. "Don't worry dear, there's other fish in the sea."

When they pulled into the airport, Danielle's heart sank. She hated to say goodbye to Karen. "Say hi to Brian for me and come back and visit again."

"I will. And I want updates. I want to know when you complete your mission with surfer boy."

"You'll be waiting a long time for that." Danielle smiled. "'Bye, Mom."

"I'm so glad I came." Marla put her hand on Danielle's shoulder. "I'm proud of you. You came here all by yourself and started your own business. I know you think I've been a terrible mother, but all I've ever wanted was for you to be out on your own and independent."

"I know." She might even miss her crazy mother a little.

Marla kissed Danielle on the cheek. "Take care of yourself. I'll be out of touch for a while. I'm going to be on a new project in Africa, but I'll give you a call when I'm back." Danielle knew it would probably be another six months before she heard from her again. Her mother flitted in and out of her life like a reckless butterfly.

CHAPTER 5

Sporadic rain kept the tourists away, and business slowed. Danielle reorganized the store and then ate dinner on her porch. The wind picked up and swayed the branches of the coconut trees. The leaves rustled and whipped around, and waves relentlessly pounded the sand. No swimmers braved the water because of the height of the surf and the undertow. Dark clouds marched closer as the storm intensified. Lightning flickered in the distance.

Danielle hadn't seen much of Sawyer lately. She'd waved to him from a distance, but avoided him as much as possible. She'd probably scared him off. She was sure he had women to pursue who were much less trouble. And at this point, a man was the last thing she needed.

Danielle went downstairs to close the shop. She moved her pieces away from the windows and cranked the metal shutters closed. After securing everything, she trudged upstairs to unpack her suitcase. She had been taking her clothes out and putting them back in since she arrived, unsure of how long she would stay. Maybe it was time to think of this as her home.

She hung her clothes in the closet and filled the drawers in the one rattan dresser. When she reached the bottom of the suitcase, she stared at the envelope that rested there. She remembered the day when she had found it in the attic of her house. The day that she learned about Xavier Hawthorne. With a deep breath, she zipped the suitcase and threw it in the closet. The past should stay in the past.

She gathered her phone, a pillow, and a blanket and settled into the hammock on her porch to watch the storm. As she wrapped herself in the blanket, her box of tarot cards tumbled to the floor. She picked it up and slid out the cards. Keeping an eye on the advancing storm, she shuffled the deck. Lightning sparked and illuminated the surging waves on the horizon. A loud crack of thunder made Danielle jump. She drew a card from the stack — the Tower. The card mirrored the scene before her. A bolt of lightning struck the top of the tower and cracked it in two. Fire burst from the windows and two people tumbled in terror into the dark sky. She Googled the card on her phone.

This card signifies a seismic shift or change. Difficult, but The Tower offers a clean slate if you have the courage to take it.

Did she possess the courage to leave her past behind? She could never forget Xavier or get over her guilt about Matt's death, but could she be strong enough to move forward with her life? As crazy as it sounded, she still waited for Xavier. A part of her believed he would come for her, that he searched for her. He drifted beneath the surface of her consciousness always — their connection unbreakable. Danielle's thoughts wandered as she listened to the storm.

The limited amount of sleep she had been getting took its toll and she fell fast asleep, her tarot cards scattered over her lap like rustling leaves.

Danielle's hair was soaked. Rain ran in rivulets down her face. She wiped her eyes to clear her vision. When lightning struck, she recognized the road – her road – in Fairview. Her house stood across the street. She immediately looked at the window where she had last seen Xavier. Empty. She tried to move, but was rooted to the ground. A motorcycle rumbled in the distance. It came into view as it sped down the road too quickly for the conditions. The motorcycle skidded and the rider flew through the air like a rag doll. He lay on the road, lifeless, one of his legs bent at an unnatural angle. The lightning strikes came fast now, around the body on the street and around her house. The sky broke apart and shattered into jagged pieces. Another bolt of lightning blazed from the direction of her house straight into the motorcyclist. The body convulsed upward, then slumped back to the ground.

A car screeched to a stop in the street. The driver opened his door and ran over to the body. He dropped his phone and begin to press on the man's sternum. Sirens blared in the background. The man withdrew his hands and the motorcyclist's chest rose and fell. He slowly turned his head on the concrete and stared straight at Danielle. She swore the eyes that looked back at her were Xavier's. She tried to run, to reach out to him, but she froze.

Danielle awoke to a crack of thunder. Her blanket weighted her down, completely drenched by the rain. Panic spread through her as she felt an uncharacteristic emptiness. The details of the dream confused her, but even more unsettling was the disappearance of the subtle ache of Xavier's presence. She knew without a doubt, Xavier was gone.

Days passed. Dreams no longer disturbed Danielle's sleep. Not to dream at all was worse than the nightmares. As her memories faded and the dreams ceased, Danielle wondered if any of it was ever real. The rain and stormy weather continued. Danielle retreated to her studio and tried to capture the images of her dream on canvas before they faded. She sketched the road and the rain, the body of the motorcyclist on the ground, his eyes that burned like small fires, and the house with its empty windows. She drew it over and over, ripping the pages from her sketchbook and throwing them to the floor. She tried to hold on to it, but the memory blurred like a reflection obscured by the rain. The remnants needled and pricked at her brain like tiny splinters.

Her memories of Xavier had anchored her. Without him, she drifted, rudderless, with no direction. Although she had convinced herself that she would never return to the house to find him, the possibility had given her some comfort. Now she knew there was nothing left there for her. She was truly alone.

CHAPTER 6

anielle tossed and turned. The sheets twisted around
her legs; her pillow crumpled into an angry blob
beneath her head. *Might as well go for a swim,* Danielle
thought. Maybe she could tire herself out enough to be able
to sleep.

She dragged her board to the edge of the water and
shoved the paddle into the sand next to her. A full moon
glowed in the cloudless sky. The surface of the water glistened. Between the light of the stars and the moon, she
could see all the way to Mona Island. From the corner of
her eye, Danielle noticed a shadowy figure strolling toward
her. Danielle recalled the stories about spirits and held onto
her paddle just in case.

"It seems we share the same affinity for midnight walks.
Can I join you?" Vanessa said.

"Sure." Danielle leaned her body away from Vanessa
and hoped she would not mention the reading.

"I haven't had such an interesting session in years. Your
connection to the spirit world is strong. Whoever wanted to

contact you was very persistent about delivering his message." Vanessa held out her hand. "May I?" she asked as she gestured for Danielle's hand. Vanessa traced the lines on her palm. "Your heart line is strong. I see a large gap here, a marriage ended?"

When she remembered Matt, she felt only guilt over his death. It blotted out any happiness they'd once had like an eclipse. And any thought of Matt immediately led to Xavier. She missed a ghost more than she missed her own husband.

Danielle snatched her hand back. "I'm sorry, Vanessa. I'm not in the mood to revisit my past tonight. I was just about to head out." Danielle rose and grabbed her paddle and board.

"I didn't mean to upset you. Enjoy your paddleboarding. But be careful, the spirits are active tonight. Take care, Danielle." As she walked away, Vanessa's skirts danced in the wind.

Danielle considered going back to the apartment, but after lugging her board to the beach, she didn't want to turn around and go home. Besides, she would never be able to sleep now. She pushed through the breaking waves to the calmer water that shimmered in the silver glow of the moonlight. Danielle's head swirled with memories of Xavier. She had to face it. He was gone. She should grow up, stand alone, and make a life for herself.

She paddled out beyond the reef. Because of the bright light of the moon, she could glimpse fish as they darted through the coral. She lay down on her board. In her rush to get away from Vanessa, she hadn't tied the ankle strap. She ignored Sawyer's voice in her head telling her to always secure the strap. Danielle closed her eyes and rocked in the dangerous cradle of the sea, oblivious to the dark clouds that gathered in the distance.

Danielle stood on the beach. Someone walked toward her out of the shadows. As the figure drew closer, she saw that it was Matt, on his shoulders a girl with bouncing golden curls. She knew without a doubt that this was their daughter. They both smiled.

"Matt, you're okay," Danielle said.

"Of course we are." Matt cocked his head to the side.

"Where are you going? Let me go with you."

"No, we're just passing through, but you need to wake up."

"I'll come with you. Don't leave." She held out her arm to grab him as he came closer.

"Danielle, wake up. Now."

She reached out to touch him and then pulled back her hand in horror. Matt's neck oozed blood from the gunshot wound. His skin withered and hung from his bones. The girl on his shoulders slid into his arms, no longer a girl, but a red and bloody fetus, limp and lifeless.

Danielle woke with a gasp, disoriented and unsure of where she was. A wave smacked into her board. She toppled off and her head thumped against a piece of the reef. As she flailed her arms and legs trying to reach the surface, a sharp piece of coral pierced her leg. The waves pummeled her and she choked as water burned in her lungs. She searched for her board, but the tide had swept it away.

Danielle tried not to panic. She couldn't be too far from shore. She could make it back if she didn't pass out. Exhausted and dizzy, she fought through the water that felt as thick as cement and willed herself to take one more stroke. Her vision blurred. She lifted her hand to her forehead and felt a huge lump forming. Her shin throbbed. She needed to rest for a little bit. Her eyes fluttered shut and she floated in a semiconscious state of emptiness — no memories, no guilt. A blank slate, she drifted into the endless darkness, enveloped in the ocean that carried her like a shroud.

A voice echoed from far away. Someone grasped her arm and dragged her onto a board. Danielle jerked fully back into consciousness when the sand scraped her back.

"What the hell did you do to yourself? Come on, wake up."

As her eyes focused, she saw Sawyer above her. Water dripped from his hair onto her face. A deep crease formed between his brows.

"Thank God." He rested his forehead on his arms. "I'm going to take you to the hospital. There's a gash on your leg that's probably going to need stiches and I'm pretty sure you have a concussion."

"No, no hospital." Danielle slurred. Hospitals meant needles, and Danielle did not do needles. She had spent a month preparing herself for a simple blood test. She glanced at her leg. Blood ran from the place where the coral had torn into her skin. Her stomach rolled at the sight.

"There's no discussion about this. You're going," Sawyer commanded. He picked her up and carried her to his truck. He placed her on the front seat and got in next to her.

Pounding pain emanated from a large lump on her head.

"Talk to me. I don't want you to pass out again. You have to stay awake." He squeezed her thigh.

"You're the Knight of Wands." Danielle pictured Sawyer atop the flowered steed on the tarot card.

"What? You're not making any sense. You must have hit your head hard."

"The tarot card, The Knight of Wands. Except you ride a truck, not a horse. You're always coming to my rescue. How did you find me anyway?"

"I was sitting on my porch enjoying the night and I saw the board wash up on the beach. I went to investigate and recognized the purple lotus flower on it. Why didn't you strap it to your ankle? You could have drowned. And what were you doing out there at night?"

"I couldn't sleep."

Sawyer shook his head as they pulled into the parking lot of the hospital.

"Do you think you can walk?"

Danielle winced as her foot hit the asphalt. He grabbed her around the waist and helped her into the emergency room. He sat in the chair next to her while the doctor examined her. As Danielle explained what happened, she knew she sounded like an idiot. Who else goes paddleboarding at midnight?

"You have a concussion, Ms. Williams, but you'll be fine. Take it easy, and come back and see us if you continue to display symptoms like headache, dizziness, or nausea. We'll give you some medication for the pain. It might make you a little sleepy. Is your boyfriend going to give you a ride home?"

"Yes, I mean no, yes...he's not my boyfriend." Danielle realized she made no sense.

"I'll give her a ride home," Sawyer said.

"Good. You'll also need stitches for that cut on your leg. We'll be back in a minute and take care of it."

"Can't I just get a Band-Aid?" Danielle pleaded.

"No, you need stitches. The cut is quite deep. I'll be right back."

"I'm going to throw up," Danielle moaned. "Either that or pass out."

"That seems to be a recurring theme for us. You sure know how to show a guy a good time." Sawyer laughed.

"I did warn you that I was trouble." Danielle immediately tensed when the doctor returned. After they flushed out the wound, Danielle tried not to look at the syringe and the rest of the instruments of torture on the silver tray.

Sawyer scooted his chair closer to the bed and held her hands in his. "I'll distract you with my handsome face."

Danielle winced as the sting of the novocaine needle pierced her skin.

"Look at me, Danielle. Concentrate on my words.

'My hands have not touched pleasure since your hands, —

No, — nor my lips freed laughter since "farewell,"And with the day, distance again expands

Voiceless between us as an uncoiled shell.

Yet, love endures, though starving and alone.

A dove's wings clung about my heart each night

With surging gentleness, and the blue stone

Set in the tryst ring has but worn more bright.'"

Although Danielle focused on Sawyer, Hart Crane's words drew her back to Xavier. She pictured wings closed around her heart. The distance between her and Xavier felt insurmountable. He existed out of her reach. The stab of another needle broke her reverie.

"This will take care of the pain. It would be good to stay with someone tonight so they can keep an eye on you. And no more paddleboarding at night," the doctor admonished.

Sawyer helped her off the bed and continued to hold her hand as they left the hospital. The pleasant haze of the pain medication took effect as they bumped over the road from town in silence. She leaned on his shoulder and absorbed the warmth and strength that emanated from his body.

Sawyer parked behind his apartment.

"Thanks for pulling me out of the water and taking me to the hospital. Maybe I'll see you tomorrow." Danielle held onto the side of the truck as she stepped down.

"No way, you're staying here tonight. You heard the doc, you need someone to keep an eye on you." Not wanting to be alone, Danielle climbed the concrete stairs. Sawyer followed behind her. At the top, he edged past her to hold open the screen door.

"I'll sleep on the couch."

"There's enough room on the bed." Sawyer yawned. "After all the excitement, I don't have any energy for any funny business, so don't worry." He checked his phone. "It's three in the morning."

"I'll sleep for a little while, and then I'll walk home." Danielle curled up on the couch, exhausted from the medication, the concussion, and almost drowning.

"Suit yourself, but if you change your mind…" Sawyer gestured to the bed.

Danielle watched through blurred eyes as he removed his shirt and shorts and grabbed a blanket from his bed. He walked over to Danielle in his boxers. She noticed a tattoo of a cross on his hip. She would have to ask him about that. As he got closer, Danielle buried her face in the cushion, not wanting to get caught staring.

Sawyer draped the blanket over her and touched her hair gently, as if she might break.

Danielle woke up trembling, her cheeks wet with tears. Visions of Matt as a corpse, the baby dripping blood in his arms, the motorcyclist dead in the road, his head slowly turning toward her, and the shock of water filling her lungs jumbled together in her dreams. Her mind swirled with a freak show of images. She was ashamed that part of her had wanted to drown tonight, thinking that might be the only way she would ever see Xavier again. Unable to get comfortable between the pain of her leg and her throbbing head, she glanced over at Sawyer who slept without a care in the world.

She crept quietly over to the opposite side of the bed and lay down at the very edge. His chest rose and fell in a steady rhythm. Unlike her, Sawyer seemed uncomplicated, untouched by any tragedy. Everyone had secrets, but so far she saw no shadows, no dark corners in him. She wished she could absorb his calm. She matched her ragged breathing to his slow rhythm.

He turned over and flung his arm out, smacking Danielle on the head.

"Ouch," Danielle squeaked.

Sawyer jumped. "Shit, I didn't know you were there. Did I hit your head? I'm sorry." He touched her forehead. "God, you're burning up. I'm going to get some ice."

"I'm all right." Danielle sat up against the headboard.

He climbed out of bed, his boxers slung low on his hips, accentuating the perfect V of his muscles. Danielle caught a glimpse of his shaft. *Karen might be right,* she mused. He returned to the bed with ice wrapped in a towel and held it on Danielle's head.

"I thought you were sleeping on the couch." Sawyer swept a strand of her hair behind her ear.

"Couldn't sleep. Bad dreams. I thought a change of location might help."

A trickle of water ran from the towel down her nose and landed on her lip. He brushed it aside with his finger. "So what really happened out there with you tonight?"

Danielle didn't know if it was the anonymity of the dark, the haze of pain medication that still muddled her head, or the comforting weight of Sawyer's hand on her shoulder, but the words flowed from her like blood from an open wound. She told him about Matt, the miscarriages, and their last fight. She recounted the details of the night of Matt's death—how she invited Xavier's brother Caleb over and how Matt took the bullet meant for her. The only part of the story she couldn't bear to retell was her affair with Xavier, a ghost. That would remain locked deep inside her.

Sawyer listened patiently, nodding his head, interrupting only a few times to ask questions.

When she finished, she took a deep breath. It had been a relief to finally tell someone the thoughts that raged inside her head. Silence permeated the air. Danielle wished she could see Sawyer's face. *Did she make a mistake opening up to him?*

"Thank you." Sawyer finally spoke. "For trusting me enough to tell me."

"At least now you know where all my sleepless nights and crazy paintings come from."

Sawyer slid his hand down her arm and took her hand in his. "I get it, Danielle, more than you know."

"Oh, come on, you're the happiest person around. I don't think I've ever seen you without a smile on your face."

"Some of us are just better at hiding our pain, but that's a story for another day."

Danielle wondered if his comments had anything to do with the cross tattoo she had seen on his hip.

"You should get some rest." Sawyer gently kissed her forehead and settled the blankets over them.

Light crept through the window as the sun began to rise. Sawyer started to snore. Knowing that sleep would never come, she quietly slipped from under the covers and limped home.

Her head throbbed, her leg ached, and a large black and blue area extended beyond the bandages on her shin. She dreaded coming face to face with a mirror and seeing the nasty bruise on her head. When she got close to her apartment, she walked to the water's edge and plunked down in the sand. Some fishermen in boats dragged their nets in search of fish, but the hush of the waves was the only sound in the early morning quiet.

Danielle felt hollow, like an empty seashell washed onto the shore, no longer a home for anything, drifting with no purpose. But then there was Sawyer. She didn't know what to make of their slowly evolving relationship. She knew there would be no strings attached—no drama, no promises, if that was what she wanted. She was drawn to him like a flower bending toward the sun, his light the antithesis to her darkness.

CHAPTER 7

Danielle avoided Sawyer thinking that perhaps she had revealed too much the night of her accident. When a late afternoon shower blew in, the beach was left deserted. Although the rain lasted only half an hour, everyone had scurried away to take cover. Caught up with her inventory in the shop, Danielle walked outside with a book and two blankets. She spread one blanket on the sand, covered herself with the other, and escaped into her book.

She had read a couple chapters when she felt a nudge at her side. She pulled the blanket from her head.

Sawyer stood above her.

"Hi, what's up?"

He sat next to her on the blanket.

"What's up? I gallantly save you from near death in the ocean and you disappear on me. I thought we had a moment there. I'm deeply wounded."

"You were very sweet to take care of me and listen to my rambling sob story."

"Sweet? My ego is crushed. I'll have to remedy that. Move over, missy." He crept underneath the blanket next to her. "How's your head and your leg doing, by the way?"

"Still sore. I think my paddleboarding days are over." She turned to face Sawyer.

"Maybe you should go during the day like normal people and with someone experienced, like me."

"I don't know, at the moment me and the ocean have a tumultuous relationship."

"Is that what turns you on? Tumultuous? Since sweet doesn't seem to be cutting it?" He leaned close and whispered in her ear. "I think I need to show you that I'm not always so sweet." Sawyer slid his hand under her bathing suit bottom and teased her with his fingers.

Danielle peeked from under the blanket and saw a few people venturing back onto the beach. "Are you kidding? There are people right there." Danielle's cheeks flushed and her heart hammered.

"They don't have X-ray vision. Just be quiet. Can you be quiet?" Sawyer challenged as he circled her clitoris with his thumb.

Danielle's inhibitions dissolved in the heat spreading down her belly. "I can be quiet, but what about you?" She countered as she ran a finger along the length of his hard rod.

"Oh, you're on," Sawyer traced her folds. "But we should make this a little more interesting." His eyes twinkled with mischief. "Whoever loses gets a tattoo."

"That's a bet that I'm not going to lose. You know I can't stand needles."

Never one to shirk from a challenge, Danielle reached beneath Sawyer's swim trunks. She squeezed his balls, then stroked his penis and caressed the sensitive tip. She concentrated on him to keep her mind off her own body. He grazed his thumb over her slick skin. He pulsed his finger in her, his pinky rubbing against her backside. She matched her strokes to his, increasing in speed and intensity. Only the sensation of their rhythm existed. Sawyer's precum moistened her hand. He groaned as Danielle gripped his rod and slid her wet fingers up and down. His pleasure tipped her closer to the brink of an orgasm. His thumb hit exactly the right spot, and she braced herself as her body contracted. She pursed her lips as the spasms of her orgasm wracked her body, but she couldn't contain a moan of pleasure as she clenched his finger. She tugged hard on his penis and he grunted loudly as he shuddered. His warm cum spread over her hand. Danielle threw the blanket over their heads, convinced that everyone on the beach was staring at them.

"Looks like we're both getting tattoos." Sawyer grinned.

"So what's new? Have you forgiven me for not telling you about your mom?" Karen asked.

"Of course. I could never hold a grudge against you. So guess what I'm doing later this afternoon?"

"I have no idea. Going paddleboarding? Reading a book?"

"I know my life is pretty boring, but no. I'm getting a tattoo."

"You're kidding. A tattoo? You? You're right, I don't believe it. With your fear of needles, you'll be passed out before you get there."

"Yeah, I kind of lost a bet."

"A bet, with who?"

"Sawyer." Danielle held the phone away from her ear as she anticipated the screech from the other end of the line.

"Sawyer! What kind of bet? You did it, didn't you? Please tell me you fucked him."

"Do you have to be so rude? Not exactly, we kind of had a thing on the beach, but it's not serious."

"On the beach? I want details. Was he huge? Was it amazing?"

"It was...good. He's a nice guy, but...I don't know, it just wasn't the same."

"The same as what?"

Danielle searched for the words to describe how she felt about Sawyer. "It was kind of like eating a whole plate of French fries. Satisfying at the moment, but afterward you feel kind of bad. Or drinking a bottle of cheap wine. It goes down easy, but the next day you feel like shit."

"My poor romantic Danielle, always looking for love."

"No, I'm done with love. I want to be on my own now, not rely on anyone else."

"Come on, I know you better than anyone else. You're punishing yourself. Give the poor guy a chance, will you? You can't keep beating yourself up over what happened with Matt. You deserve some fun. Let me know how the tattoo goes and send me a picture. And keep me posted on any developments with hot surfer dude."

"I will. I'll talk to you soon."

Danielle mulled over what Karen had said. Maybe she should give Sawyer a chance. She searched under a pile of mail until she found the business card he had given her the first day they met. She put in his number and composed a text.

Want to come over for a drink before we get our tattoos?

Danielle scrunched her face and held her breath as she hit Send. She chewed her fingernails as she waited for his response.

Danielle fluttered around the apartment, her nerves on overdrive. She changed her clothes four times, made her bed twice, turned the music on, then off, then on again. "Get it under control, Danielle," she muttered. She had not been on a date in seven years, although she wouldn't really consider this a date. It was just a drink, after all. She grabbed her phone and decided to blast her go-to song for stress relief — "I Don't Fuck with You" by Big Sean. She cranked up the volume and started singing at the top of her lungs.

The sudden appearance of Sawyer at the top of the stairs interrupted Danielle's chorus.

"I knocked, but you didn't answer, so I just came up. Interesting song choice you got going on there. Hope that wasn't meant for me?" Sawyer smirked.

Danielle's cheeks reddened. "Just you know, killing time until you got here." *God, he was hot*. He looked like he just got out of the shower, his damp hair pulled back into a ponytail, the thin t-shirt he wore unable to conceal the curves of his washboard stomach.

Sawyer grabbed Danielle's phone from the table. "Let's see what else we can find here. Now how about this?" "Mandy" by Barry Manilow started to play.

"Oh, classic. I forgot you're a Manilow fan."

"Who isn't?" Sawyer placed her phone down and extended his hand. "Let's dance."

"Who wouldn't want to dance to this?" Danielle raised her eyebrows.

Sawyer pulled her close, his arm around her back. She trembled under his touch.

He whispered in her ear, "So did you really ask me over here for a drink?" He pulled away to look at her face.

Danielle parted her mouth to speak, but no words came.

Sawyer leaned forward and pressed his lips to hers. His tongue gently probed as he crushed his body to hers. He gripped her head and tangled his fingers in her hair. She could feel his hardness against her as she wound her arms around his back, pulling him even closer.

She wanted this, wanted to lose herself with Sawyer, their bodies the only thing that mattered.

"I've wanted to do this since the first time I laid eyes on you at the bar," Sawyer murmured.

Danielle couldn't help but smile.

Sawyer slid her dress off her shoulders as he kissed her neck, her shoulders, her breasts. Danielle pulled off his shirt, marveling again at his ripped abs. She pressed her lips to his chest, her hard nipples brushing against his skin. Sawyer moaned, his face burrowing in her hair. Danielle pulled him toward her bed.

"Wait," Sawyer said. "I'll be right back." He walked into the kitchen and opened her freezer. He walked back holding an ice cube between his thumb and finger.

Danielle scrunched her forehead in confusion.

"I've been fantasizing about this ever since the night you were in my bed."

Danielle felt the tightening in her belly as she imagined what Sawyer might have in mind. He pulled her onto the bed and lay next to her.

He traced the ice cube over her lips, her neck, and the mound of one breast. He circled her nipple with the ice cube and continued down to her belly. He skimmed over the hem of her underwear to her clitoris where he swirled the ice cube. Her abdomen contracted.

He scooted aside her underwear and slipped the ice cube underneath, massaging her clit with the ice cube and his fingers. An unbearable mix of the cold of the ice and the heat of his skin caused wetness to spread between her folds. When the ice melted to a tiny piece, he withdrew his hand and pulled off her underwear. He retrieved a condom from the pocket of his shorts before taking them off.

Danielle raised her eyebrows. "Was I that obvious?"

"You said a drink, but a man can always hope." He ripped open the packet and took his time as he rolled it down his large shaft.

He nestled between her legs and lowered his head to kiss her neck. His chest grazed her hard nipples. Danielle twined her legs around him and held onto his shoulders. Sawyer's hand reached below to finger her as his mouth found hers. His tongue teased her in rhythm with his finger.

As he entered her, Danielle clung to his back. He rode her, sweetly and gently at first, until she moaned for him to go deeper and grabbed his ass to pull him closer. Sawyer quickened his pace. He filled her until she clenched and shuddered against him as he came inside her. Sawyer showered her face with kisses before he slid from her and lay on her side.

Danielle couldn't help but smile as she looked at Sawyer. With him next to her, she felt like there would be no room for the darkness, no way for the past to push through his light.

As they walked to Tattoo Nation, Danielle considered what kind of tattoo to get. She wanted something to symbolize her new start, her new life. The waves lapped at her feet and the sky burst into red, orange, and yellow as the sunk sank. The gulls flew, their wings spread wide as they glided effortlessly. At that moment, Danielle knew a wing would be the perfect way to mark her past and symbolize her flight into this new life.

Her steps slowed as she approached the shop. "Please don't let me pass out." She whispered prayers to whatever god might be listening at the moment.

"Getting cold feet?" Sawyer asked. "We don't have to do this, you know."

"No, I'm good. I'm ready, but you do realize there is a distinct possibility that I may pass out during this. Me and needles…not so good." The color drained from Danielle's face as she envisioned the sharp metal piercing her skin.

The shop buzzed with the sound of all the equipment.

"You'll be fine. Angel is a pro and I'll even hold your hand if you want me to." Sawyer smirked. "Hey, Angel, are you ready for us?"

A man covered in tattoos from head to foot looked up as he finished with another customer. "Give me a minute and I'll be right there," Angel said.

While Danielle and Sawyer waited, they flipped through a book of designs on the counter.

"I'm going to get this wave on my shoulder. What do you think?" Sawyer asked.

"I love it. Then you'll always have the perfect wave with you."

"How about you?"

Danielle turned the pages in the book. "This one, a wing. On my back, that way I can't see what they're doing."

"So what can I do for you guys today?" Angel came from around the counter and hugged Sawyer. "Good to see you again, *amigo*."

"You too. So, I'm going to get this wave and Danielle is going to get a wing."

"Good choices." Angel nodded. "The wing seems to be very popular. A guy came in here yesterday who got the same tattoo, on his neck though."

Danielle shivered. Xavier. Every corner she turned, another reminder ambushed her. She existed in a constant tug of war between the past and present.

"Let me get your paperwork. You can pay Charlotte over there and we'll get things ready for you. I'll be doing your tattoo, Danielle, and José will be doing yours, Sawyer."

Danielle hoped she wouldn't embarrass herself and cry like a baby.

"All set. Come on over to my chair, Danielle. Sawyer, you can go to the next chair."

As Angel explained the process to her, Danielle tried to keep her breath steady by repeating in her head, don't pass out, don't pass out—her own personal mantra. She lay face down on the chair and turned toward Sawyer who joked and laughed with José.

Angel cleaned her back and applied the stencil to her skin.

"We're ready to start. Take slow, deep breaths. *Lista*? The first couple of minutes will be the worst."

"Yup, go ahead." Danielle braced herself and closed her eyes. She flinched at the first stab of pain.

"I promise it will get easier." Angel talked very little after that as he concentrated on his work.

Danielle clenched her hands, determined not to let the pain win. As Angel etched the tattoo, she imagined each line seared one of her sorrows into her skin. A line for the miscarriages, one for Matt, and the deepest for Xavier. Her memories burned. She hoped she could leave them there, behind her.

"We're all done. You did great. I'm going to put ointment on and cover it. Leave the bandage on for at least three hours. No swimming for two weeks until it heals."

Danielle nodded, surprised that Angel had finished already.

"Do you want to see it before I put the bandage on?" Angel handed her a small mirror.

"Sure." Danielle walked over to a large mirror at the back of the tattoo parlor. The image of the wing yanked her back to the past, to the first moment Xavier's face hovered above her, the tattoo wrapped around his neck, his lips as they brushed hers. Danielle turned her back on the reflection.

Sawyer walked over from the counter, his shoulder already bandaged. "I knew you could do it! Let's go celebrate." As they set out for the Playa Bar, he grabbed her hand. For the first time, Danielle didn't feel the urge to pull away.

After ordering two beers, Sawyer lifted his bottle.

"To tattoos, bets, and…friends." Sawyer hesitated on the last word. They clinked their bottles and drank. "I'll be right back. I want to talk to Desireé about the surfing report."

"No problem, I'll be right here."

"You and Sawyer both got tattoos today?" Leisa asked. "Please tell me they're not matching ones."

"Of course not. I have a wing, and Sawyer got a wave."

"Huh. A guy came in a little while ago. He had a wing tattoo, but it was on his neck."

The hair on Danielle's arms stood on end and her heart raced like a ticking time bomb. "A wing tattoo on his neck? What did he look like?"

"Shaved head, dark skin, buff body. Hot, model material. He's still here, over in the corner."

Danielle held her breath. For a moment, she hoped beyond hope for Xavier. *So much for putting the past behind me.*

A man sat in the corner hunched over his drink. Definitely not Xavier, but Leisa was right, he could be a model. She licked her lips as she imagined sketching the curves of his muscles. His skin looked like dark velvet. A wing tattoo wound around his neck.

He raised his head and their eyes met. An explosion of neurons fired off a million sparks in her brain. She felt as if she knew him, should know him; but she didn't, she couldn't. His eyes, his face…she could swear it was the face of the man on the motorcycle from her dream, Xavier's eyes, but that wasn't possible.

The man gripped the sides of the table so tightly, she could see the veins in his arms. Danielle tore herself from his gaze and put some money on the table for the beers. The last time she followed her intuition it had ended in a tragic, tangled mess. She refused to go down that road again.

"Tell Sawyer I'll be down at the beach."

"No problem," Leisa replied as she scurried around to get ready for the dinner crowd.

As Danielle walked down to the steps to the beach, she noticed Vanessa sitting at a table. A sign advertised free tarot readings. *I know I shouldn't do this, but what the heck.*

Danielle walked over to the table and sat down.

"Good to see you again, Danielle. Would you like a tarot reading?"

"Sure."

"Perfect, let's do a three-card spread. Shuffle the cards for me, please." Vanessa handed her the deck.

Danielle shuffled the cards. Her pulse quickened as she handed them back.

"Now cut the deck."

Danielle lifted a section off the top and placed it on the table.

Vanessa pulled three cards and placed them in front of Danielle.

She turned the first one over. "Three of Swords, pain and disappointment and hurt are in your past. You've endured great sorrow and loss."

Danielle nodded in agreement; so far, nothing new. She took a deep breath as Vanessa turned over the next card.

"Your present, the Hanged Man."

Danielle sighed and shook her head. On the card, the man hung upside down from a gallows, a halo of sun around his head. *I can never do anything the easy way.*

Vanessa continued. "Don't be deceived, this is a wonderful card. The Hanged Man symbolizes transformation and change. It's a chance to view life with a new perspective. You are like a caterpillar who waits in her cocoon until she is transformed into a beautiful butterfly, ready to take flight."

"So I'm a caterpillar. I guess it could be worse." Danielle shrugged.

"And now your future." Vanessa flipped the last card. "The Five of Wands. Interesting. This card signifies conflict within yourself. You must decide if you will follow your head or your heart."

Is being with Sawyer following my heart? As she mulled over the meaning of the last card, Danielle felt a hand on her shoulder.

"Leisa told me you were going for a walk. Ready to go?" Sawyer asked.

"Sure. See you later, Vanessa. Thanks for the reading."

"Anytime. You should stop by my shop. We could do something more in depth, maybe a Celtic Cross spread. It might help give you some answers."

"Maybe I will."

Danielle got up and reached for Sawyer's hand. She was ready—ready to leave her past behind and start over. As they walked down the beach hand in hand, Danielle pictured herself with wings, darting above the waves, free from memories, soaring into the future.

FROM THE AUTHOR

Thank you for reading *Eight of Cups*! If you enjoyed it, I would be thrilled if you would consider telling a friend or leaving a review. For updates and news about upcoming books, visit my website, www.JDBrettonWriter.weebly.com, follow me on Twitter @JDBrettonWriter, find me on Facebook, or connect with me by email at BrettonJD@gmail-com. I'd love to hear from you!

J.D. Bretton

In the Major Arcana, The Hanged Man symbolizes sacrifice, surrender-and finally, rebirth.

Danielle has left behind the nightmares, the longing for her old love, and fears of a new love. Will Sawyer be her rebirth? Will the mysterious man bring sorrow? Or will she return to her old love Xavier?

Coming next summer: read the conclusion of Danielle's journey in *The Hanged Man*, Book 3 in The Tarot Trilogy.

www.ingramcontent.com/pod-product-compliance
Lightning Source LLC
Chambersburg PA
CBHW070534130626
46555CB00003B/1415